# SESAME STREET STORYBOOK

## No More Milk
Illustrated by Edward Koren

## Fisher-Man
Illustrated by Joseph Mathieu

## Fire-Man
Illustrated by John Trotta

## A Lot of Hot Water
Illustrated by Stan Mack

RANDOM HOUSE

# No More Milk

It was a beautiful day on the farm.

The cherries were ripe, the flowers were blooming, the corn was growing...

...the sun was shining, and the grass was green.

But over by the barn, sitting on a stool, was a very sad man.

He was the man who took care of the cows.

He milked the cows twice a day, every day of the week.
He milked them on Monday, on Tuesday, on Wednesday.

He milked them
on Thursday,
Friday, Saturday,

and on Sunday.

This man's name was Milk Pail Peters.

Milk Pail Peters. That's what everybody called him.
And most of the time, Milk Pail Peters was very happy.
He loved to milk his cows and take the nice fresh milk
to the dairy so that everybody would have good milk
to drink.

Well, when everyone saw how sad Milk Pail Peters was
now, they went to him and asked him why he was so
unhappy. The tears came out of Milk Pail's eyes. He
told them that his cows would not give milk. He had
tried and tried and tried and *tried*, but his cows refused
to give him any milk. Now poor Milk Pail Peters did
not know what to do.

Then someone asked him if he was ever mean to the cows. No, thought Milk Pail Peters, he was always nice to the cows... except maybe yesterday.

Yesterday morning Milk Pail Peters had gotten out of bed and stepped on a tack. The tack hurt his foot, and that made him very angry.

When he went to milk the cows, he was still angry. So he yelled at the cows and pulled real hard for the milk.

Now, the cows didn't know that Milk Pail Peters had stepped on a tack. They hadn't done anything to Milk Pail Peters. Yet there he was yelling at them. And that's when they stopped giving milk.

Now Milk Pail Peters knew what he had to do. He had to do something nice for the cows so that they would forgive him and let him milk them again. So he hopped up and ran out to the pasture and went right up to the Head Cow, who was just standing there minding her business and chewing her cud.

"Head Cow," said Milk Pail Peters, "I'm going to let you and all your sister cows have all the grass you want."

Well, the Head Cow kept right on chewing her cud. She didn't even look up . . . the cows already *had* all the grass they wanted.

Then Milk Pail Peters said, "Head Cow, I'll give you sunshine in the summertime, snowflakes in the winter, flowers in the spring, and pretty leaves in the fall."

The cow kept chewing her cud.

Milk Pail Peters didn't know what to do. "I'll give you water from the creek," he shouted. "I'll give you clover, and birds to sing for you."

The cow turned around and walked away, chewing her cud like she didn't even hear him. Poor Milk Pail Peters sat down in the pasture. What could he do for the cows? He did not know. He did not know.

Just then, at that very moment, who should come walking across the pasture but one of the smartest men in the world. And they called this man Common Sense Sanders. Common Sense Sanders! He could figure out almost anything. Boy, was Milk Pail Peters glad to see Common Sense Sanders!

Milk Pail said, "Hello, Common Sense!"
Common Sense said, "Hello, Milk Pail! What's wrong with you?"

Milk Pail said, "Common Sense, yesterday morning I yelled at the cows. I pulled hard to get their milk. And now they won't give me any more milk. I offered them sunshine and snowflakes, grass and clover, fresh air, and everything! And they wouldn't even listen to me!"

Common Sense Sanders thought for a minute. Then he asked, "Did you apologize to the cows?"

"What?" asked Milk Pail Peters.

"Did you apologize? Did you tell them you were sorry you yelled at them?"

"Well, no. I didn't think of that."

"Try it," said Common Sense, and he walked away.

Milk Pail Peters wasn't sure what would happen, but he thought he'd try it. He caught up with the Head Cow, and he said, "Head Cow, sit down a minute and let me talk to you." And the Head Cow sat down.

"Yesterday, when I pulled real hard to get milk from you and your sisters, I was very angry. I wasn't angry with you, I was angry because I had stepped on a tack, and I am so sorry that I took it out on all of you. I am *so* sorry, Head Cow, that I feel like leaving the farm forever and never coming back. I am *so* sorry, Head Cow, that I can hardly stand here and talk to you without feeling *so* ashamed of myself that I want to crawl in the nearest gopher hole and tell my troubles to the nearest gopher. I am so sorry, Head Cow, that I…"

But before Milk Pail could go on, the Head Cow got up and held a meeting with her sister cows and as quick as you could say "Common Sense Sanders" . . . there was milk all over the pasture.

Not only was there regular white milk, but by some

kind of magic there was buttermilk, chocolate milk,
heavy cream, light cream, ice cream, eggnog, and butter,
and everything else you could make out of milk.

And there stood Milk Pail Peters. He was still sad.
Why? He had forgotten to bring his milk pail.

# FISHER-MAN

Way way out in the middle of the ocean, on a rainy, rainy day, there was a fishing boat. It was the only boat for miles around, and the name of this boat was the Bad Ship Sloppyslop. The Bad Ship Sloppyslop —the sloppiest, dirtiest, grimiest, filthiest boat on the seven seas.

Everywhere the Bad Ship Sloppyslop went—on the ocean, on the seas, on the rivers, on the lakes—the crew dumped garbage and trash overboard. They made the waters dirty for fish and dirty for people. The captain of this boat was Greedy Grimes.

Now, if you think the Bad Ship Sloppyslop was bad, you should have seen Greedy Grimes. He was worse than the ship. And the worst thing about Greedy Grimes was the greedy way he fished. You see, Greedy Grimes and his two crew members, Trapping Travis, the lobster lover, and Sardine Davis, the small-fish man, lived on a little island called Dumb Dumb Island, just the three of them. But, when they went fishing, they caught hundreds and hundreds of fish, many many more than they needed.

Why, Greedy Grimes would catch big fish like tuna and swordfish.

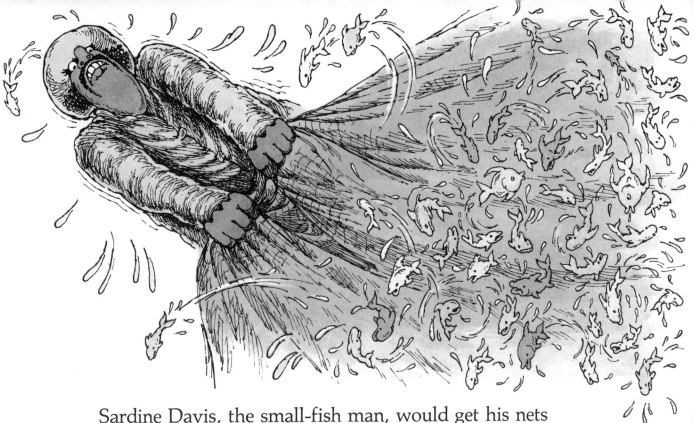

Sardine Davis, the small-fish man, would get his nets
filled with sardines and smelts and all kinds of little
fish. And Trapping Travis, the lobster lover, would set
hundreds of lobster traps everywhere he even *thought*
that he could find a lobster.

PRACTICALLY NO LOBSTERS IN THIS AREA!

Now, on this rainy, rainy day, Greedy Grimes was sure that the Bad Ship Sloppyslop was the only boat on the ocean, so he tried to catch every fish swimming and crawling. He and his cruddy crew caught bass and flounder and crabs and mackerel and eels and everything they could reel in and pile on board. And to make room for more fish, they threw all kinds of junk in the water. They tossed in tin cans, old papers, orange peels, old rubber tires, just plain junk and garbage— anything to make room for more fish.

They piled so many fish on top of the boat that something began to happen. Something began to happen! The Bad Ship Sloppyslop began to sink. There they were in a sinking boat, way way out in the middle of the ocean, with the wind blowing, the rain pouring, and not another ship for miles around. When Greedy Grimes realized that his boat was sinking because the fish were too heavy, do you think he threw his fish overboard? Do you think so? No! He was too greedy! He just stood there and yelled and hollered, "Somebody, somewhere, save my boat and save the fish I caught!"

Of course, there was only one man in the world who could save him. Only one man. And that man wore a gray costume with a wide black cape, and a great pair of boots, and a black leather hat with a mask over his eyes, and they called that man Fisher-Man. Fisher-Man! Fisher-Man lived in the bottom of the ocean in a two-story watery castle, and he was there to make sure that no one made the water dirty and that no one took more fish than he needed.

Naturally, Fisher-Man had no use for Greedy Grimes and he wasn't too happy about the Bad Ship Sloppyslop or Trapping Travis or Sardine Davis. But, when a boat was in trouble, even if it was the Bad Ship Sloppyslop, it was Fisher-Man's duty to save the boat and everybody on board. So, when Fisher-Man heard Greedy Grimes yelling and hollering, he zoomed through the water until he came to the sinking ship.

28

Right away, Fisher-Man knew what to do.
He jumped on board the Bad Ship
Sloppyslop and took all of the fish and
put them back into the ocean. Then the
ship was not as heavy as it was before,
so it stopped sinking and floated safely
on top of the water again.

But instead of being happy that they were safe, Greedy Grimes and his crew were angry because all of their fish were gone.

"Fisher-Man," said Greedy Grimes, "you had no right to throw all of our fish back into the ocean!"

"You're wrong, Greedy Grimes," said Fisher-Man. "Your boat was sinking because you had too many fish. Now! Not only won't you get your fish back, but I'm going to get all of the garbage and junk that you've ever thrown in the water and put it back on your boat."

Then the fantastic Fisher-Man scrounged up all of the junk in all of the water in the world and piled it all on top of the Bad Ship Sloppyslop. And in one great movement, he picked up the junky boat with one hand and swam back to Dumb Dumb Island. There he dumped the boat, the junk, Sardine Davis, Trapping Travis, and right on top of this huge pile, Captain Greedy Grimes himself.

And there they all are to this day, living in the Bad Ship Sloppyslop, up on top of all that garbage, and wishing they were someplace else.

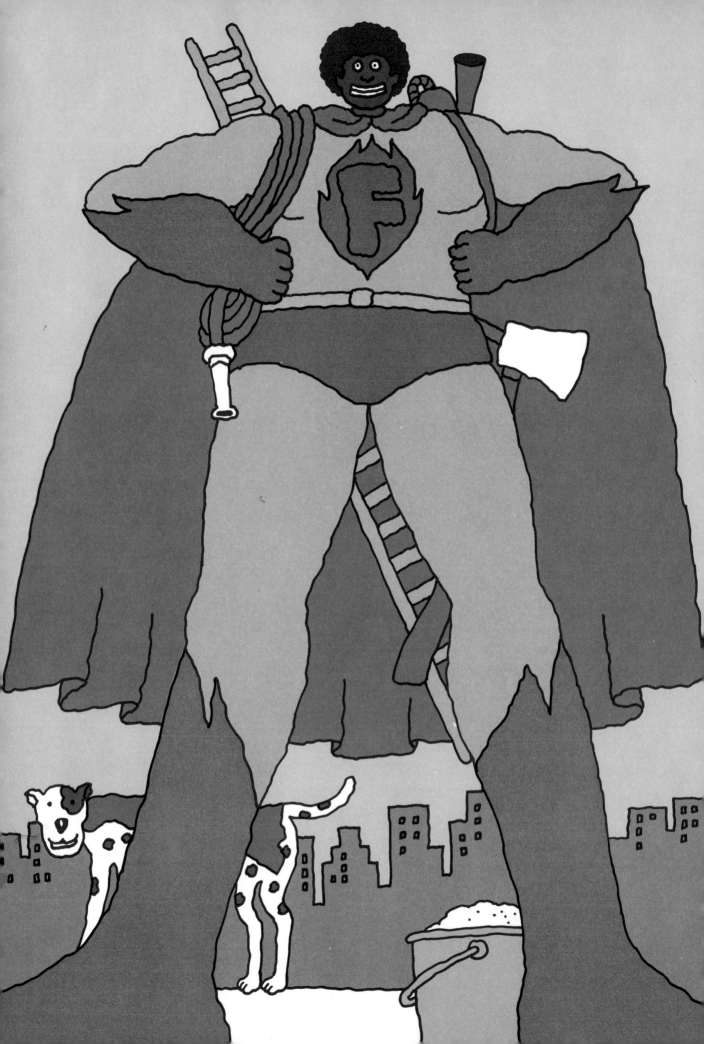

Now, you may have heard of Fisher-Man. I know
you've heard of Batman and Superman and Hawkman
and Sandman. But have you ever heard of Fire-Man?
Fire-Man! What a man. What a man! Now, Fire-Man
was not the kind of fireman you see on a fire truck
going to put out a fire. Oh, no. He was very different.
He spent all of his days and all of his nights making
sure that little boys and girls did not play with fire.

Fire-Man wore a tough green uniform with a big red letter F on the front, and whenever he found out about a little boy or girl playing with anything that might start a fire, he strapped on his great purple fire extinguisher, his big blue bucket of sand, and his 5,000-foot hose, and flew off to keep the children from burning themselves.

Now, everybody was happy when Fire-Man was around. Children loved to watch him and his faithful Dalmatian, Five Alarm, flying by. They loved it when he came to tell them about all the things they shouldn't play with—things like stoves and furnaces and plugs and sockets and especially matches.

But no one knew much about Fire-Man. No one knew why he was always on the lookout for fires or why he cared so much about keeping little children from being burned. That's because no one knew much about the World's Worst Day!

It happened when Fire-Man was a little boy. Everybody called him Freddie Firebug then. Freddie Firebug, because he loved to play with fire.

On the World's Worst Day, Freddie Firebug was at home by himself, and he was down in his basement, sitting in a pile of old rags and newspapers that he had stacked up against the furnace. He was playing with a pack of matches, striking every match in the pack, and throwing each one up in the air just so he could watch the fire fly. Soon he was tired of that, and he lit all of the matches, threw them over his shoulder, and walked away.

Little Freddie Firebug then went upstairs to the kitchen.

When he got there he decided to fry a hot dog. So he poured some oil in a pan, threw a hot dog in, and turned on the stove.

Then he decided to do something else, so he walked into the living room, and when he got there he saw the socket on the wall where the lamp was plugged in. Freddie Firebug also saw a hairpin that belonged to his mother. He wondered what would happen if he stuck his mother's hairpin into the socket.

He pulled the plug out of the socket, then very slowly he stuck in the hairpin. Nothing happened. He stuck it in a little further, and further, and further, until all of a sudden sparks came out, and Freddie Firebug felt the worst pain he'd ever felt in his life! His hand was stinging and hurting and aching and burning!

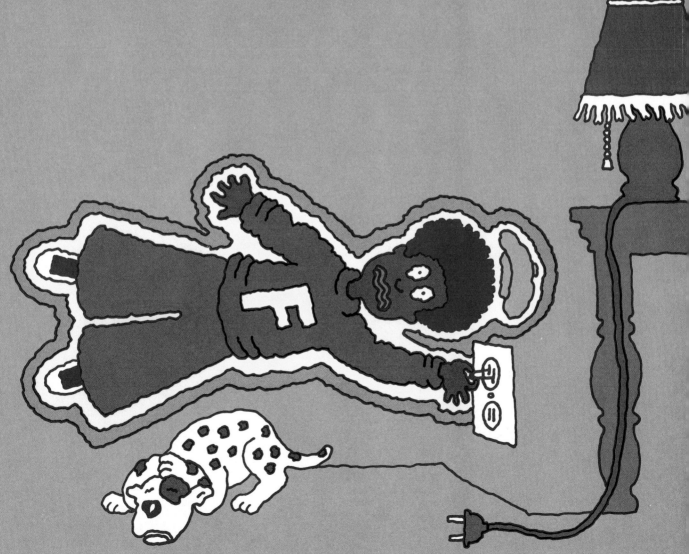

Freddie Firebug screamed and cried, and ran into the bathroom to run some cold water on his hand, but the water didn't help. It still hurt.

He ran to the kitchen for some ice, but when he got
to the kitchen there was nothing but smoke and more
smoke. The hot dog was burning and the pan was on
fire.

Freddie Firebug ran out of the kitchen and headed toward the basement. But fire was coming from the basement—great big red, yellow, orange, blue, and green flames whipping up the steps.

Freddie screamed and cried. His hand hurt from the socket shock, he choked on the smoke from the kitchen, he was getting hotter and hotter from the fire in the basement. He didn't know what to do.

Just then, his father rushed in and grabbed Freddie and carried him out of the burning house.

The fire trucks came and the firemen tried to put out the fire, but the fire was so big and so hot that by the time the fire was out, the house was nearly burned to the ground.

It was the World's Worst Day, and it taught Freddie
Firebug a lesson. He wanted to teach that lesson to all
the little boys and girls in the world. So, right then and
there, as Freddie looked at his burned-down house, he
promised that when he grew up he would become the
greatest fire fighter in the whole universe. And he did.

And that's how Freddie Firebug became . . . FIRE-MAN!

# A LOT OF HOT WATER

There once lived a very old man who didn't like people. And they called this man Lonesome Lewis.

Lonesome Lewis was his name, and he didn't mind being lonesome. He liked it. He lived alone. He had no books. He had no radio. He had no television. He had no newspapers.

He also had no one to help him when he needed help, but that didn't bother Lonesome Lewis. He told everyone in the world to go away and leave him alone.

He loved being lonesome.

Now one night, after Lonesome Lewis had been by himself all day, he decided to take a bath before going to bed. So he turned on the hot water until the tub was filled.

Then, when he went to turn the water off, he found that he could not do it. He could not do it. He turned and he turned and he turned, but he could not turn it off.

The water kept running and running, and soon the tub
was running over. Lonesome Lewis had troubles now.
The water was over the faucet and when he reached in
to turn it off, the water was so hot that it burned his
hand. But that didn't stop Lonesome Lewis. He ran out,
got a glove, and put the glove on his hand so that he
wouldn't feel the hot water.

But he still couldn't turn it off, and
pretty soon the hot water soaked right
through the glove, and his hand was
hot again. He yanked his hand out of
the water, and by now he thought he
should call Hot Water Williams, the
plumber.

But he was Lonesome Lewis, and he had to do things by himself. So he wrapped a washcloth around the glove on his hand, and he put his hand back into the water, but he still couldn't turn it off. And now the water was all over the bathroom floor.

Oh, he knew he should call Hot Water Williams, the plumber, but he had to do things by himself. He had to keep on trying till he got it.

This time Lonesome Lewis put a towel around the washcloth around the glove on his hand, and he stuck his hand back into the water, but he still couldn't turn it off. And the water went through the towel, through the washcloth, through the glove, and Lonesome's hand was hot again. And this time he looked and saw the water running all over the hall and onto the rugs and everywhere.

Now Lonesome Lewis knew he had to have some help, so he ran to the phone to call Hot Water Williams, the plumber.

But then he remembered something. He didn't like people, so he didn't have a phone. And if he didn't have a phone, how could he call Hot Water Williams?

And the tub was still running over. The hot water ran down the hall. It ran down the stairs. It burned Lonesome Lewis's feet.

"Ouch!" yelled Lonesome Lewis.

When Lonesome Lewis yelled that "Ouch!" people
99 miles away could hear it.

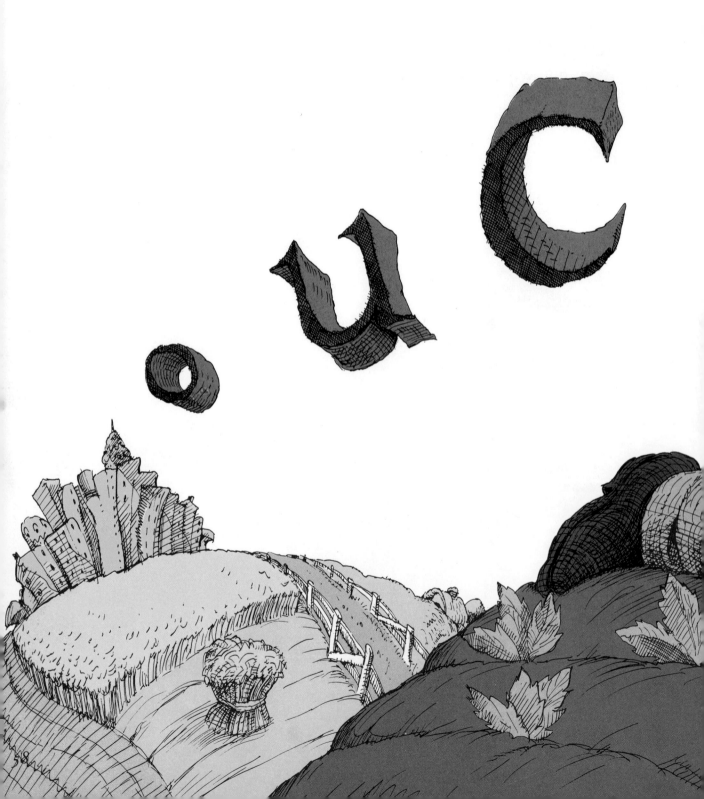

59

Now Lonesome Lewis was really worried. He knew he had to fix that tap by himself, so he grabbed all the towels he could find, and his bathrobe, and some old socks, and all the washcloths and everything in sight.

He wrapped everything around his hand to keep the hot water from burning him.

But when he stuck his hand in to see how hot the water was, much to his surprise the water was cold. You see, all of the hot water had run out. Now Lonesome Lewis knew just what to do.

He reached all the way down in the water and pulled out the plug.

Most of the water went down the drain, and now Lonesome Lewis got a good grip on the faucet and turned and turned until he finally turned it off.

But what a mess there was. What a mess! Everything was soaked, and there was so much to clean up! Just then, the doorbell rang.

A lot of people had heard Lonesome Lewis's yell. They knew he was in trouble, and even though they knew that he didn't like people, they came to help anyway. Lonesome Lewis opened the door. And there was Wet Mop Weaver, who came in and mopped up all the water.

And Clean-Up Clayborne came in and cleaned up all of the towels and gloves and wash-cloths and everything.

And there was Hot Water Williams, the plumber, who went right to the bathtub and fixed that hot water faucet once and for all.

And when everyone was finished, they said good-by.

And Lonesome Lewis started to ask them to wait and stay with him for a while . . .

. . . but he decided to let them go and to stay by himself, because he was Lonesome Lewis and that was the way he was.